DEAD SCARY
ZOMBIE ROAD

TJ DOOM

Illustrated by
Nahum Ziersch

PENGUIN BOOKS

DEAD SCARY
ZOMBIE ROAD

PENGUIN BOOKS

UK | USA | Canada | Ireland | Australia
India | New Zealand | South Africa | China

Penguin Random House Australia

Penguin Random House Australia is part of the Penguin Random House group of companies whose addresses can be found at global.penguinrandomhouse.com.

First published by Penguin, an imprint of Penguin Random House Australia Pty Ltd, in 2025

Cover and internal illustrations by Nahum Ziersch
Cover design by Rebecca King © Penguin Random House Australia Pty Ltd
Internal design by Caroline Lee © Penguin Random House Australia Pty Ltd
Typeset by Midland Typesetters, Australia

Printed and bound in Australia by Griffin Press, an accredited ISO AS/NZS 14001 Environmental Management Systems printer

NATIONAL LIBRARY OF AUSTRALIA

A catalogue record for this book is available from the National Library of Australia

MIX
Paper | Supporting responsible forestry
FSC www.fsc.org FSC® C018684

ISBN 978 1 76135 289 8 (Paperback)

We at Penguin Random House Australia acknowledge that Aboriginal and Torres Strait Islander peoples are the Traditional Custodians and the first storytellers of the lands on which we live and work. We honour Aboriginal and Torres Strait Islander peoples' continuous connection to Country, waters, skies and communities. We celebrate Aboriginal and Torres Strait Islander stories, traditions and living cultures; and we pay our respects to Elders past and present.

A WARNING

Dear Reader,

The Dead Scary books aren't like any others.

They're twisted. They're spooky. They'll make you laugh and scream – sometimes at the same time. Most of all, they're exciting. Once you start, you'll never want to put them down.

But before you dive in, a warning.

Scary stories are strange things. The more you read, the more they stay with you. They creep into your mind, curl up in the shadows and whisper to you when the lights go out.

But you're brave. I can tell.

So go on, turn the page.

If you dare.

Sleep tight,

TJ DOOM

ABOUT THE AUTHOR

TJ DOOM lives off the grid in a crumbling mansion at the edge of a dark and windswept forest. Surrounded by creepy old portraits that appear to watch – and judge – the writer's every move, DOOM spends the long, haunted nights crafting sinister stories designed to do just one thing: mess with your head.

DOOM's tales are precision engineered for maximum dread. Some say that if DOOM's books are cracked open after midnight, the creatures inside won't just haunt your dreams, they'll crawl out of the pages and come looking for you.

TJ DOOM doesn't do interviews. Doesn't sign autographs. Won't even pose for a photo. Naturally, this has fuelled rumours that the writer is an ancient, blood-sucking vampire whose image can never be caught on camera.

Because DOOM is always uncontactable, this cannot be confirmed.

Or denied.

CHAPTER ONE

ACE Walker wishes he was as cool as his name sounds.

He's not the leather-jacket-wearing, motorbike-riding rebel you'd expect from someone called 'Ace'. He doesn't swear. He doesn't talk back. And he most definitely *doesn't* ride a motorbike. No, he's a twelve year old who never does anything wrong. He's a good kid. His mum says it all the time.

'Ace, you're a good kid.'

And he likes that; he likes being the good kid. So, he always finishes his homework on time. And eats his vegetables. And stacks the dishwasher. And never, ever, ever stays out after dark.

Because when the sun goes down, *they* come out.

So, you stay inside.

Or they'll find you.

And eat your brains.

Every night since the eclipse two years ago, Ace has heard them. Shrieking just outside the house in Red Rock where he lives with his mum, Diane.

Located in the middle of a desert, Red Rock is a one-horse town – population: 414 – though there are actually two horses and they both live on a tiny ranch *outside* of town.

Ace knows the area like the back of his hand because after school, but before the sun drops below the horizon, he makes deliveries for his mother, who cooks and sells meals from their kitchen. Simply, he's the town's Uber Eats driver, except he rides a bike and doesn't work for Uber.

That's another reason he's a good kid. Ace works for his mum after school instead of playing sport. He'd really like to play football one day, but he just doesn't have the time.

Sylvester, his dad, loved football. Ace thinks he would have wanted him to play, would have taught him everything he needed to know about the game. But that never happened because a year before the eclipse, when Ace was nine, Sylvester went out to buy a carton of milk one morning – and never came home.

His father used to talk about travelling the world, of having grand adventures in far-flung countries, crossing deserts and climbing mountains, visiting cities he'd only seen on the internet. And he made it sound like something they'd do *together*, as a family. Ace never imagined he'd go without them. With no warning. And no goodbye.

'Order up!' That's Ace's mum. She's just cooked and packaged another meal and now he has to ride it over to the Pohlers' place. He glances at his watch. He has plenty of time. It's only 4.57 p.m. and the sun won't set until 6.54 p.m. The round trip shouldn't take him more than twenty minutes, as long as he gets a hustle on.

As Ace collects the large brown paper bag full of his mother's delicious homemade pasta and garlic bread from the kitchen bench, he notices she has that melancholy expression she sometimes gets.

Ace knows the look pretty well. A lot of times they'll talk about why she feels sad, which he knows makes her feel better, though occasionally, like now, he doesn't have time. So, he does the only thing he can: he makes a heart shape with his hands and presses it to his chest. He understands it's a poor stand-in for real words, but his mum knows what it means: that he loves her and he'll be the good kid she needs him to be.

Outside on the verandah, Ace zips the bag of food into the insulated carrier on the back of his bike, then pulls on his helmet. He understands that the leather-jacket-wearing, motorbike-riding rebel version of Ace would never wear a helmet, but the idea that he could have a stack, hit his head, be knocked out and then wake up outside *after* sunset, when *they have risen*, is enough to make sure he wears it every single time.

The ride out to the Pohlers' place is easy-peasy.

It's pretty hot, but it's a dry heat, which has always been Ace's favourite kind of heat. And he finds the warm breeze that rolls off the desert in the late afternoon refreshing on his face. There's hardly any traffic on Red Rock's main street at the best of times, but by late afternoon, most people have headed home for the evening, so he has the road to himself.

Once he makes the drop at the Pohlers', who love his mum's cooking and always tip him well, he heads home. He's about five minutes away and hoping he won't need to make another delivery when he notices something on the road.

At first, he thinks it's a clump of clothing, like someone was on their way to the laundromat but got jack of it and just dumped their washing in the middle of the street. Then he rides closer and realises it's an actual person.

And not just any person.

It's his best friend, Cassie Waites.

A15 Larkspu
STORE

CHAPTER TWO

'CASS!'

His heart hammering, Ace leaps off his bike, sprints over and drops to his knees beside her. 'You okay?' He's very relieved to see her eyes blink open. 'Did you get hit by a car?!'

Cassie looks up at Jake, pain carved into her face. 'No. I was crossing the road – but didn't make it to the other side.' She half smiles. 'That sounds like the beginning of a joke, except I don't feel very funny at the mo.'

Ace exhales, happy she hasn't been the victim of a hit-and-run, but still confused as to why she is lying in the middle of the street. 'So, what's wrong?'

'My tummy,' she murmurs. 'Pain. Is. *Sooo*. Bad.'

Ace winces in sympathy as his gaze moves to her hands, which are tightly clutched over her stomach. 'What is it?'

Cassie's voice falters. 'Don't know. But it hurts to talk. So I'm gonna shut up now.'

Ace nods, his mind racing. Should he get her off the street? Or call Doc? He remembers hearing something about not moving someone who's sick because it might make things worse, so he pulls out his phone. 'I'm calling Doc.'

She nods faintly and Ace dials Doctor Ramsey. Since the eclipse that changed everything, Doc's number has been in the phone of every person in Red Rock. Either that or they had it committed to memory. You just prayed you never had to use it.

The phone rings and is picked up. 'You got Doc.'

'Doc, it's Ace. Ace Walker.' Ace tries to keep his voice grounded and steady so not to cause alarm. In his experience, panicking never helped anything. It just made everyone freak out.

'What can I do for you, son?'

'My friend, Cassie – I think she's sick. Her stomach is really hurting. I've never seen her like this before.'

Doc's friendly tone instantly shifts and he's all business. 'Where is she now?'

Cassie groans. It's not very loud, but it's loud enough.

'Hear that?' asks Ace.

'I did,' replies Doc. 'Where is she?'

'I found her lying in the middle of Main Street.' Ace glances at the nearest intersection to get his bearings. 'We're near Cove Road.'

'Be there in a sec.' Doc hangs up. And Ace knows he *will* be here in a sec, because everything is only seconds away in Red Rock, as long as you have a car. Unfortunately, Ace is still five long years away from getting his licence, though his dad taught him the basics of safely operating a motor vehicle as his eighth birthday present.

Ace turns to Cassie. 'Doc'll be here in a sec.'

She nods again, but this time it's like the very act of partially moving her head up and down is the most painful thing she has ever attempted.

Ace takes Cassie's hand in his and tries to look braver than he feels.

This is the girl who saved his life.

Twice.

The first time was when she showed up for him after his dad left. She just hung out at his place like nothing was wrong and never got bored or annoyed that he wasn't exactly a hype beast to spend time with. She let him be sad and angry without making it weird and that, more than anything, got him through what was a pretty trash time in his life. He's always been grateful for that and wonders how he could ever pay her back. Maybe now's the time.

It's only a matter of minutes before they hear the low, V8 rumble of the doctor's faded blue Ford pick-up. There are no ambulances in Red Rock. Or hospitals. Just one doctor with an old truck and a small surgery in a simple room at the back of a modest house.

The truck skids to a halt beside the kids, and in a flash, Doc is out. He's about the same age as Ace's mum and a good-looking rooster. He doesn't have a wife, so Ace often wonders if he might be interested in dating Diane, hoping that might make Ace's mum feel a bit less sad. But it hasn't happened yet, even though Ace thinks they have a vibe.

Doc kneels beside Cassie. 'How are you?'

'You're not catching me at my best.' She tries to keep it light but immediately regrets the pain of speaking.

'So, your stomach hurts, huh?'

She nods faintly.

'Where, exactly?'

Cassie points to the right side of her stomach, down low. Doc tries his best to keep his expression neutral, but Ace is sure that he saw a slight grimace ripple across his face. 'Is it a sharp pain or a dull pain?'

'Sharp.' It takes a lot of effort to get the word out. 'But it was dull before.'

No hiding *that* expression. Doc definitely grimaced. 'Okay, well, let's get you in the back seat.' Doc turns to Ace. 'I'm going to need your help.'

Ace nods, and together they slowly but gently haul her to her feet. Cassie groans once but is very brave.

'I've got her.' Doc nods at the truck. 'Get the back door.'

Ace does as he's told and together they slide her inside so she lies across the back seat. Ace grabs his bike and swings it into the truck's tray, then climbs in beside Cassie.

He moves a long black umbrella with a thin metal tip to the floor so he can reach the seatbelt, which he carefully loops around her, doing his best not to touch her stomach. In a flash, Doc is behind the wheel and driving them to his surgery, which is just a couple of minutes away.

As they go, they pass house after house, all of them similiar, suburban and ordinary at first glance. But looking closer, Ace sees the steel bars welded over windows, the doors reinforced with metal plates and the fences lined with iron spikes. They aren't just homes anymore; they're fortresses, braced to repel the things that come out in the dark.

Three minutes later, Ace and Doc ease Cassie out of the back seat. She sags between them, groaning softly as they slowly guide her towards the surgery at the rear of Doc's house.

Ace can feel heat radiating off Cassie and realises she's burning up. 'What's wrong with her?' He half-whispers, half-mouths the question to Doc.

'You know I can hear you, right?' mutters Cassie.

Doc doesn't sugarcoat it. 'Appendicitis.'

Ace's stomach drops. 'How bad?'

Doc meets his eyes, and his grim expression says it all.

Bad.

Ace glances west. The sun is falling fast, bleeding orange across the sky. He checks his watch. Yes, he wears a watch. Not because it's old-school cool but because he can't trust a phone. Too easy to lose, drop, smash, or for it to run out of juice just when you need it most. A hand-wound watch is much less likely to fail. And that's important because he always needs to know the time. That, and when the sun will set. So, first thing every morning, he scribbles that time on his forearm, right beside his watch. Today, in black marker, is printed: 6.54 p.m.

It is currently 5.59 p.m.

They reach the rear of the house. 'I don't feel fantastic,' whispers Cassie, her voice barely audible.

'You're going to be fine. Just hold on.' Ace says it like he believes it. He's not sure he does.

Doc unlocks the surgery's heavy, metal-plated door and shoulders it open with a grunt. Inside is a plain, sterile room painted that gross hospital green that looks like spinach threw up.

They lower Cassie onto the examination table, Doc's face slick with sweat from the effort of hauling her in. He crosses to a drawer and pulls out a box of painkillers, the same kind Ace's mum takes if she has a headache. He pops out two tablets and passes them to Cassie. 'These will help with the pain.'

Cassie dry swallows them both before he can fetch her a glass of water.

'They'll take about half an hour to kick in.' Doc then places his fingers on Cassie's stomach and presses gently.

Cassie flinches.

Doc's expression tightens and he presses again, a little harder this time.

Cassie lets out a sharp gasp.

That's all Doc needs to know.

'So, it is my appendix?' Cassie asks through gritted teeth.

Doc nods.

Ace leans in. 'So you need to leave like, *right now*, don't you?' Ace knows full well that Red Rock is not built for a medical issue like this. There's no emergency room, no surgeons, no nothing. Whatever's wrong with Cassie, this dusty old town can't fix it.

Doc doesn't answer as he checks his watch. Ace can see the gears grinding behind his eyes, running the numbers, weighing the odds.

The nearest hospital is in Larkspur. Population: 1637. A towering blue cross adorns its roof and is lit up at night like a beacon of hope for those in need of healing.

Unfortunately, it's ninety-two kilometres away.

Ninety-two!

If Doc floored it in his old truck, held a steady one hundred and fifty clicks an hour, he could make it in forty-three minutes. That's fast for an 1980s rust bucket. And technically illegal too. But no-one enforces the traffic laws out here. Not since the eclipse.

So, if Doc left right now, and nothing went wrong, he'd beat the sunset – still forty-nine minutes off, according to Ace's trusty watch.

But that's not the problem.

The problem is the road.

Most of it's a thin, unsealed scar that's all sharp gravel and jagged potholes that wants to shred your tyres and break your heart. One blowout and you'd better know how to change that wheel quick smart because when the sun drops, they *rise*. And out here, that's not just bad luck.

That's a death sentence.

It's why Ace has heard one thing over and over since the eclipse.

You never drive to Larkspur after dark.

Cassie groans again, her breath ragged and rough, like cloth tearing. Ace turns to Doc, desperate to know. 'So, are you taking her to Larkspur?'

Doc doesn't move. Doesn't blink. Just stares into the distance, the sweat glistening on his face. Ace wonders if he's still crunching the numbers – then he notices the look in his eyes.

Distant and glassy.

Something is wrong.

Very wrong.

Doc stiffens and his hand flies up to grab at his chest. His mouth opens like he's about to speak, but no words come. Instead, he topples over – and hits the floor hard.

'Doc!' Ace scrambles over and kneels beside him. His fingers fumble for a pulse at the neck.

Nothing.

'Oh no, no, no – Doc!' Ace frantically places his hands on the doctor's chest, locks his elbows and begins compressions.

Steady.

Measured.

Exactly how he was taught at school.

One. Two. Three. Four. He counts in his head, each press precise and deliberate.

Thirty compressions.

He feels Doc's neck.

No change.

Ace tilts the doctor's head back, pinches his nose shut and then gives two controlled breaths into his mouth.

'Breathe, Doc! Breathe!'

CHAPTER THREE

CASSIE stirs, her voice a slurred whisper. 'What's happening?'

Ace doesn't answer, just keeps on with the compressions, trying to pace them evenly as panic claws at him. 'Breathe! *Please.*'

Ace feels Doc's neck again.

No pulse.

No breath.

No life.

No Doc.

He's dead, Fred – and there's nothing Ace can do about it.

Poor guy.

When the sun sets, the dead rise. And that will happen in forty-eight minutes. And Doc will be one of them. Poor guy.

Lovely Doc, who had done nothing in his life except selflessly help other people. Ace wonders if it's terrible that one of his first thoughts is how disappointing it is that Doc will never ask Diane out.

It astounds Ace that you can live a good and noble life and never hurt a fly, then die of wholly natural causes, and the *very next evening* you'll be up and prowling the streets, looking to satisfy your newfound taste for brains with any live human you can sink your teeth into.

Cassie tries to lift her head, but it's too painful. 'What's happening?' She sounds groggier than before.

Ace moves to the examination table where she lies. 'Doc collapsed.'

'Is he okay?'

There's no easy way to say it. 'Yeah, naaah. It would seem he's – gone.'

'I don't – what?' Cassie is confused. 'Gone where?'

'I guess, to heaven?' But Ace doesn't believe that. He doesn't think anyone goes to heaven. Not since the eclipse.

'What?' Then Cassie turns and sees Doc's body on the floor. 'Oh god!' Her voice cracks. 'What happened?'

'Pretty sure it was a heart attack.'

Ace can feel the panic rising in Cassie, and in himself too, but he can't afford for them to go there. Not now. Not with time bleeding away. So, he does the only thing he can. He pivots. Hard.

'How's your stomach?' he asks, too fast, too loud, like if he changes the subject quickly enough, reality won't catch up.

Cassie flinches, her hand pressed to her side. 'Bad, man. So bad.' She winces as the words leave her lips.

Ace takes this in – then makes a decision. 'We need to get you to the hospital.'

Cassie nods. 'Call my parents.'

'Where's your phone?'

'Back pocket.' Ace gingerly slides it out of her jeans pocket, only to find that the front glass is shattered from when she collapsed on the road. The phone is unusable, so he grabs his.

Cassie recites the number and he calls Bernie, Cassie's dad, on speaker. It rings and rings and rings – then goes to voicemail. Ace leaves a message and tells him Cassie isn't feeling well and Bernie needs to call back ASAP.

Cassie isn't surprised he didn't pick up. 'Try Mum.' She winces as she says that too, then relays her mother's phone number.

Ace nods and calls Margarette, hoping she'll answer. Again, it rings and rings and rings – then goes to voicemail. He leaves the same message as before.

Ace sees the pained expression on Cassie's face and knows it isn't just about her appendix. It's the disappointment of having not one but two hopelessly unreliable parents. Not only are they terrible at picking up the phone, but they've also been terrible at everything else, including picking her up from school when she was little. She usually came home with Ace.

Cassie's not this independent by choice. Her parents were never very attentive to start with, but then came the eclipse, and with it, the loss of friends and family. It hollowed them out, and whatever part of them that cared about other people slipped away. So, Cassie was left to look after herself. And that's where Ace and his mum stepped in. They became her chosen family.

Right now, Cassie tries to be brave, as she always does, but her face crumples. 'I don't want to die, man.'

'I will *not* let that happen.'

She hears it but it doesn't look like she believes it. Then she starts to spiral. 'I haven't done anything with my life.'

'You're *twelve*. *Nobody's* done anything with their life at twelve.'

She looks at him, eyes wide and searching. 'What am I going to do?'

'*You* don't have to do anything because *I'm* taking you to the hospital in Larkspur.' Ace doesn't hesitate for a second. It's settled and he can't think of a better way to repay her for being such a good friend.

She can't quite believe it. 'Are you sure?'

'Of course.'

She's so relieved. 'Thank you, thank you.' Then she thinks. 'How do we get there?'

'Doc's truck. It's right outside. And he's not going to need it.' Ace glances at his watch. Forty-five minutes until sunset. 'But we have to go *right now*.'

'Then what are we waiting for?' Cassie does her best to grin through the pain.

'Okay, up you get.' Ace helps her off the table. It's a slow and laborious process, and her whole body trembles from the effort, her face twisted in a mask of agony. Ace loops his arm around her back and helps her towards the surgery door, gingerly guiding her around Doc's body.

They both try not to look at it. Ace thinks, after all the death they'd seen these past few years, they should be numb to it by now. But they're not. He's pretty sure you never really get used to it –

Schrieeeeeeeeeek!

Doc's corpse releases a blood-curdling sound then shudders.

'Ohhh geez!' Ace flinches and Cassie stumbles. She just manages to stay on her feet as Doc's mouth flies open – then slams shut.

Snap!

The sound echoes across the room like a gunshot. Then Doc's lips peel back in a grotesque caricature of a grin while his hands spasm, each finger bending at an extreme angle, twitching and clawing at the air like a spider flipped on its back.

Ace and Cassie recoil as the dead man's legs convulse with sudden, violent kicks. Then his spine arches sharply and lifts his torso impossibly high off the floor –

CHAPTER FOUR

Doc's body slumps back down with a heavy thud then lies still.

Ace knows it won't stay like that for long.

The doctor formerly known as Doc isn't one of the undead *yet*, but something deep inside him has started to shift and change. His body is already reshaping and reconstituting itself for what comes after sunset.

Ace's heart thunders in his chest. 'So, that was horrible.'

Cassie looks even paler than before. 'For reals.'

They both exhale a shaky, anxious breath, then quickly shuffle outside, where it's noticeably darker now.

Cassie gestures to Doc's beaten-up old truck. 'You know how to drive this thing?'

Ace nods. 'Absolutely.'

That is a barefaced lie.

Ace has never driven anything like this vehicle before. But desperate times call for desperate measures. He's seen adults do it plenty of times, so how hard can it be?

They reach the truck and Ace pulls open the rear door and gently eases Cassie into the back seat, just like before. She slumps across it with a groan, then turns and gives Ace a thumbs-up. He pushes the rear door shut, jogs around to the driver's side and climbs in.

The keys are in the ignition, just like he knew they would be. Doc always left his keys in the car in case he needed to go somewhere fast. In fact, everyone in Red Rock used to do that, until they started to worry that some zombie might remember how to drive.

Ace fastens the seatbelt, which is a bit loose because the retractor seems to be broken, then realises he's way too far from the truck's controls.

So, he faffs around with the seat until he finds the right position. Thankfully he's tall for his age and can see over the dash.

He twists the key and the truck's engine turns over – but doesn't fire. 'Come on.' He tries again and the big V8 rumbles to life. He releases the handbrake, drops the gear lever into drive, finds the accelerator pedal with his foot, and taps it. With a grunt, the old truck jolts forward like it's been woken from a bad dream.

'Ahhh!' Cassie cries out from the sudden movement.

'Sorry!' And with that, Ace gently presses the accelerator and steers the truck towards the street at the end of the short driveway –

Brrrrrrrrrrrrrrrrrrrrrrrrrrrrrrrrrrrrrrrrr!

A deafening horn splits the air as a massive semi-trailer barrels straight towards them –

Ace's eyes go wide and he slams the brake pedal with both feet. The tyres scream and the truck skids – and stops *just* before the street as the road train blasts past, a wall of steel, rubber and noise that misses them by three inches. The wind it kicks up rocks the truck like a hurricane.

Cassie groans unhappily from the sudden jolt of the emergency stop.

'That's on me!' Ace takes a deep, steadying breath, looks both ways to make sure there isn't another road train bearing down on them, then gently touches the accelerator again. The truck rolls forward.

The street is completely empty.

Ace checks his watch.

Forty-two minutes until nightfall.

They lost three minutes getting in the truck, adjusting the seat and then avoiding the loud and scary road train. So, they need to get a move on to make up time. There can't be any more delays.

Ace grips the wheel tight and floors the accelerator. The truck doesn't leap forward so much as lumber. The engine moans, then coughs and stutters to life. Ace makes a turn, then another, then, up ahead, he sees the on-ramp to Larkspur. It's about thirty seconds away –

BRRRRRRTT!!
SKREEEEE

His phone buzzes. He pulls it from his back pocket, drops it on the passenger seat and glances at the screen.

Cassie's voice rises from the back. 'Is that your mum?'

Ace nods. 'Yep.'

'You gonna answer it?'

'If I do, she'll tell me to come home. So, I'm not going to answer it.'

Cassie smiles, part in relief, part in disbelief that someone is doing this for her. 'Thanks,' she says softly.

'No worries. Don't ask for permission, ask for forgiveness, right?' It's something his dad used to say. Ace realises this is the first time he's ever tried it.

Ace will call his mum when they reach the hospital in Larkspur to explain the situation and say sorry. Then he'll drive back at sunrise and take whatever punishment is coming. If she's mad – and she will be – he'll wear it. Because Cassie's life matters more than a few days of trouble.

The old truck picks up speed, pushing sixty, seventy, eighty, way past the town's limit of fifty. Ace hates breaking the law, but there's no-one else on the road and the clock is ticking.

Ace glances back at his friend. The second time Cassie saved his life was just before the eclipse, after a once-in-a-generation rainstorm. They had biked out to the old Hester place to look at a paddock that had become a raging creek, running hard and fast through the back boundary before crashing into the river. Ace thought he could cross it. The water was only waist deep, after all.

Bad idea.

A quarter of the way across, the current yanked his feet out from under him. He hit the water hard, then his head hit something else even harder. It was an old fence post hidden just below the surface.

He doesn't remember the rest.

Cassie does. She saw it happen, saw him go under. No cry for help. Just gone, like he never existed. She dived straight in.

She caught his foot just before he was swept into the river. She dragged him out of the water with nothing but sheer will, then slapped his face and yelled at him to wake up and, when he did, she laughed with relief.

It was from that day on that Diane looked at Cassie in a different light. She already liked the girl, but saving Ace sealed it. She wasn't just Ace's best friend anymore; she was family, the kind you choose.

On the left side of the road, Ace spots Clem Alpine sitting on his porch as they barrel past, the old man's eyes narrowing like he knows something's off. Of course he'll recognise the truck – everyone in town knows Doc's faded blue clunker – and he'll quickly realise Ace isn't supposed to be driving it. Or anything, for that matter, considering he's only twelve, but Ace isn't slowing down to explain. He doesn't have time.

So, Ace keeps his foot down on the accelerator as they rocket up the on-ramp. The tyres hum and the engine throbs and, just like that, they're on the highway to Larkspur. Officially, it's named Section Connector 9.

But no-one calls it that.

Out here, it has only one name.

Zombie Road.

CHAPTER FIVE

ACE exhales and allows himself a smile.

They're on their way.

The first stretch of the road is paved and sealed and as smooth as a freshly shaved Timothée Chalamet on a publicity junket. It's a straight shot through the desert, right up to the Crimson Dunes that rise in the distance, stark against the blood-orange sky.

There's no traffic.

No cops.

And if they're lucky, no nightwalkers.

Ace treads on the accelerator a little harder. The engine growls, then the old truck grudgingly picks up speed. At one hundred and twenty, it starts to rattle, as if it just remembered it doesn't like to run this fast and needs to complain about it.

Ace settles into his seat, hands gripping the steering wheel tightly, eyes locked on the long, empty ribbon of road ahead. Then it hits him – something he forgot. Something critical. 'Damn it.'

He didn't check the truck's fuel gauge.

His mother used to say it all the time, to herself mostly, but as a warning to him when, eventually, he was allowed to drive. 'Always make sure you have enough petrol. *Always*. At least half a tank. You never want to run out of petrol and get stranded after dark.'

'How could I be so stupid?' Ace mutters this under his breath so Cassie doesn't hear it. No need to freak her out because he's an idiot. There's a service station halfway to Larkspur, but what if they don't have enough to make it that far?

For a second he hesitates, afraid to look at the fuel gauge. If it's low, they'll have to double back to Red Rock, and that will absolutely kill their timeline. Then he realises ignoring the problem will only make it worse, so he forces himself to look –

Half a tank!

Maybe a little more.

A wave of relief washes over him. That's plenty. They'll make it just fine. 'Thank you, thank you, thank you.' He mutters that under his breath too.

His eyes flick to the sun. It continues its slow but undeniable track towards the horizon. Then he glances at his watch. Thirty-nine minutes before that burning orb falls behind the Earth – and something else rises.

Something dark and terrible.

They're currently doing one hundred and twenty kilometres an hour, but that won't be fast enough to beat the sunset. He needs to be at one-fifty, at least. So, he presses down on the accelerator again. The old truck's V8 rises in pitch as the vehicle increases its speed. Very slowly. One-fifty-five finally shows up. Then, quite a spell later, one-sixty makes an appearance.

Outside, the road blurs like a smear of grey beneath tyres that howl and thrum. The steering goes light, almost floaty, like the truck is barely touching the ground. The slightest twitch of the wheel will send it flying off the tarmac, so he keeps his hands rock steady so that doesn't happen.

Ace really doesn't want to be out in the darkness. He's only done it once in the past two years – and that was the night of the eclipse.

He'd been playing Fortnite at Cassie's and lost track of time. When his mum called, he grabbed his bike and headed home. The eclipse was happening, he knew that much, but he hadn't really thought about it. He'd seen one before, so it felt like old news.

Still, he caught the beginning of it as he rode past Red Rock's one and only cemetery. And if he hadn't seen what happened with his own eyes, he would never have believed it.

The dead – or, more correctly, the *un*dead – rose from their graves like something out of *The Last of Us*, except playing a video game was the furthest thing from the minds of these rotting creatures.

Some of the bodies had only been buried for a few weeks. Others, years. Still others had been in the ground for decades, centuries even. But that didn't matter.

When the eclipse came, they *all* rose.

How did it happen?

Scientists later spoke of a freak gravity spike brought on by the eclipse and a rogue solar flare that both happened at the exact right – but for humanity, very wrong – moment. They called it a Goldilocks Event because everything had to be *just right* to wake the dead, just like with Goldilocks and her porridge.

Now, these weren't the shambling, slow-moving zombies you see in a lot of horror flicks. No. They were fast. And strong. And focused on one thing.

To hunt the living and feast on their brains.

Okay, maybe that's two things, but either way, once a victim's brains were devoured, they joined the zombie ranks and, in the most twisted version of the 'circle of life' imaginable, developed *their own* craving for brains.

Out of a population of 550, Red Rock lost over one hundred and thirty people that first night. Of course, it could've been worse. The undead are quick and strong, sure, but most of them are as dumb as toast. Weird, considering brains are their favourite food. A barricaded door or a boarded-up window will bamboozle most of them because they can't work out how to get it open.

Also, a gunshot will slow their roll. But it won't stop them. Nothing will stop them – except fire.

They fear the flames.

Somehow, the undead intrinsically know that if they burn, it's game over. That's why Ace always carries his late grandad's Zippo lighter in his front pocket, fully fuelled and ready to go. You just never know when you might need to light up a nightwalker.

Off to the left, Ace can see the distant Crimson Dunes fast approach. Their beginning marks the point where the paved and sealed part of Section Connector 9 gives way to the gravel road.

As the sun rose after that first night, the zombies retreated. No-one knew where they went. The cemetery was empty, so they hadn't gone back to the place where they'd been buried. It took weeks, and a number of covert operations by a small but dedicated posse of Red Rock townsfolk, to follow them before sun-up and realise they'd made a home in the Crimson Dunes.

Since the eclipse, thousands and thousands of the undead have been drawn to those towering dunes, and not just from Red Rock, but from towns far and wide. They dig themselves into the sand and hide until sunset.

Some call it their nesting ground. Others say it's like a zombie hotel. Ace calls it Motel Z, while Cassie refers to it as a Dead & Breakfast. Whatever you name it, it's where the nightwalkers hide during the day.

There was an attempt to blow up one of the dunes to take out the zombies within, but that did nothing except create some twisted, otherworldly glass sculptures from the melted sand. There was also an effort to dig out the creatures, but they were in too deep, and if they sensed movement above, they would slither away like worms through dirt and evade capture.

The town quickly learned that when the sun slipped below the horizon, doors were bolted and windows were barricaded. The night belonged to the dead now – and the living had better stay out of their way.

The old truck leaves the paved and sealed section of the road and in an instant the smooth hum of the tyres vanishes, replaced by a rough, bone-rattling rumble as gravel spits up and pings off the undercarriage like shrapnel in a gunfight.

Ace ignores it. He stays focused on the road ahead and keeps the steering wheel steady. No sudden moves. Not on this surface. It's just so slippery. The last thing he needs is to lose control and wreck the truck.

The Crimson Dunes are just a hundred metres off the road to the left. Seeing them up close, Ace understands their name. When the setting sun hits them at just the right angle, they cast a fire-red glow – and look like they're drenched in blood.

The sun drops fast. One minute it's blinding in the rear-view mirror, the next it's gone, replaced by the deep eeriness of twilight. The temperature plummets as dusk settles in, and the sky deepens from a bruised purple to a cold, hard navy. Ace flicks on the truck's headlights, which carve pale tunnels of radiance through the gloom ahead. He then cracks the driver's window slightly to let in fresh air, but not too much because he doesn't want to hear the buffeting wind inside the cabin.

He glances at his watch.

Thirty minutes to sundown.

He allows himself another smile. His plan is working nicely. They're making good time and will get to Larskpur with minutes to spare –

Bang!

The truck shudders violently. Metal groans as it skids to the right like an invisible hand is shoving it off the road. Ace instantly reacts and yanks the wheel left –

But he takes it too far. Tyres scream and the truck fishtails wildly as its rear whips back and forth.

It's like riding a dragon with one wing.

Then it happens.

The left side lifts and the truck begins to tip.

Ace's breath catches in his chest.

This is it.

If the truck flips, it's game over.

Even if they survive the crash, they'll never make it back to Red Rock on foot before sundown.

CHAPTER SIX

ACE'S instinct takes over.

Something deep in his gut tells him to turn the wheel *towards* the skid, not away from it. He's pretty sure he saw it in a film he watched with his dad.

Maybe it was one of *The Fast and the Furious* movies? He can't remember exactly, and it doesn't actually matter, but he does it and the tyres bite into the gravel. Then the truck jolts back onto all four wheels – then settles.

Ace stamps on the brake. The truck howls in protest as the speed washes away and it grinds to a stop. A moment later, a choking cloud of dust catches up with the truck and obscures his view. It's like the road is exhaling in relief.

Which is what Ace does. He glances back at Cassie. 'You okay?'

She raises a hand and gives him the thumbs-up.

'Good.' Ace knows nothing is actually 'good', because he has a pretty clear idea of what caused the bang that set the truck fishtailing.

He waits a moment for the dust to clear, then eases his foot off the brake and prods the accelerator. The truck rolls forward, but nothing feels or sounds right. There's an ominous thumping noise from the rear and the steering is sloppy and weird.

Ace stops the truck and gets out. Both tyres on the driver's side are fine. Then he circles around to the passenger side and sees it.

'Far out.' He says it low so not to freak out Cassie.

The rear left tyre is shredded and as flat as a pancake, with a chunk missing that looks like a great white shark took a bite out of it. Ace stares at the damage unhappily. That's what happens when you kiss a jagged rock doing a hundred and sixty.

He's going to have to change the tyre. His eyes flick to the west, where the sun dips behind the horizon, then he looks at his watch.

Twenty-seven minutes until sundown.

His dad used to say every young man must have a basic set of skills. They need to know simple self-defence. They need to know how to cook three tasty, nutritional meals. And they need to know how to change a tyre.

Only now does Ace realise his dad taught him all that stuff by the time he was nine, like he knew he wouldn't stick around.

'What's going on?' Cassie's faint voice drifts to Ace from the back seat and yanks him out of the memory.

He tries to keep the answer upbeat. 'Just have to change a tyre.'

'Oh.' Even though her voice is muted, he can hear her concern.

'Don't worry. Only take a sec.'

It won't take a sec.

At all.

It'll take at least ten minutes, probably more. And it'll put them behind schedule. This is what Ace was worried about back at Doc's surgery. It wasn't just the length of the trip, it was about having enough time up your sleeve in case something went sideways.

Something like *this*.

He must be quick. The dark approaches, and nothing good comes with it. So, he hurries to the truck's tailgate and swings it down. Inside the tray is a chaotic mess. Apart from his bike, there are ladders and rolled-up tarps and golf clubs and paint tins and folded deck chairs and even a green jerry can attached to the side, all of it jammed together like a junkyard puzzle.

Thankfully, the spare tyre is there too, with the vinyl toolkit roll beside it. Ace scrambles into the tray and muscles the tyre upright. It's way heavier than he expects, but he grits his teeth and rolls it to the end of the tailgate. Then it wobbles and slips from his grasp –

'No!'

The tyre drops off the tailgate, hits the gravel with a thud, then bounce-rolls away. Ace leaps off the truck and sprints after it, gravel spitting under his shoes. But the tyre is weirdly fast, like it's trying to escape. It takes all Ace has got, but he finally grabs it. When he looks back at the truck, he realises it's a hundred metres away.

'What the?!' Breathing hard, he rolls it back as fast as he can.

How much time did *that* waste?

He reaches the truck, yanks the toolkit from the tray and drops to his knees beside the shredded tyre. He unrolls the kit and grabs the wrench then locks it onto the first lug nut and pushes down to loosen it so he can get the wheel off the truck.

'Ahhh!' The lug nut does not move. Not even a bit. 'Really?!' He throws all his weight onto it and tries again.

The lug nut does not move. He realises it may have been holding this tyre in place for *years*. Then a sliver of fear turns in his chest.

What does he do if he can't change the tyre?

'Stomp it.'

Ace looks up to see Cassie's pale face framed by the rear window. 'What?'

'The lug wrench,' she says. 'Stomp it – like you're starting a motorbike.'

Ace's eyes snap to the wrench, still jammed on the stubborn lug. She's totally right. He jumps up, braces himself, then stomps on the wrench.

Crack. The lug nut turns.

'Yes! You're a genius.' Thrilled, Ace glances back at Cassie. Her face has vanished from the window, but her faint voice rises from the back seat: 'I know.'

In a flash Ace has the wheel off, wrestles the spare into position then lifts it up to push it on –

He misses.

He tries again.

No.

He's *rushing*. That's the problem.

Go slow to go fast.

His dad used to say it all the time. Rushing leads to mistakes and mistakes slow you down. So, Ace takes a deep breath to chill out then repeats the advice to himself: 'Go slow to go fast.'

He lifts the wheel – and slides it on.

'You little beauty.' He checks the horizon. Three-quarters of the sun is gone. Then he glances at his watch.

Ten minutes to sundown.

Ten?!

Where did the time go?

Ace grabs the first lug nut – and drops it. 'Go slow to go fast,' he mutters, picks it up, threads it on.

It jams.

'Why?!' Panic rising, he checks inside the lug nut.

It's full of sand!

He blows it clean and tries again. This time it spins on nice and smooth. As do the next three. Relieved, he lowers the truck and prepares to tighten the lug nuts –

Schrieeeeeeeeeek!

The distant sound shreds the still air. It's high-pitched and ragged and yet somehow guttural at the same time, infected with an inhuman hunger so raw and insistent that it makes the hairs on Ace's neck stand up and his chest buzz with a sick, electric panic.

The horrific sound can only mean one thing.

The zombies are awake.

He checks his watch.

Five minutes to sundown.

They're early.

The zombies are *early*.

And Ace is *late*.

CHAPTER SEVEN

SCHRIEEEEEEEEEEEK!

Another one echoes across the dunes.

And this time it's closer.

The sound is not quite a scream and not quite a screech, but an unholy combination of the two. It's the cry of the undead; those doomed to wander the darkness for all eternity as they hunt for the brains of the living to feed on.

Ace's eyes flick to the horizon. The sun is gone and the sky's orange glow fades fast.

Schrieeeeeeeeeek!

The awful sound is even closer now. Then comes another, this one deeper. That's a *second* zombie. They're waking up and crawling out of their sand-dune beds to search for a human stupid enough to be out after dark.

A human like Ace.

'Time to go, man.' He hears Cassie's frail voice from the truck's back seat.

'I know.' Ace takes yet another deep breath to steady his nerves, then carefully fits the wrench over a lug nut and tightens it.

One down and three to go –

Schrieeeeeeeeeek!

That one is much nearer, echoing across the dunes then bouncing off the flat side of the old truck.

Ace keeps turning the wrench, tightening the lug nuts one by one.

Go slow to go fast.

He doesn't say it aloud. He doesn't want those shrieking creatures to hear him. Word on the street is that the undead have a dog-like ability to hear. Ace is not sure why being dead improves your hearing (if you had bad hearing when you were alive, wouldn't you have bad hearing when you were a zombie?) but that's the working theory.

So, he keeps his mouth shut as, finally, he tightens the last nut. He'll be in the truck and driving away within fifteen seconds –

Schrieeeeeeeeeek!

Now that sounds *very* close.

Like, from the dune right behind him.

Ace pulls the wrench off the final nut – but does it too quickly. It slips and slams into the truck's wheel arch.

Clang! The noise reverberates across the night.

This time, there's no shriek. Instead, a different sound cuts through the dark. The one you never want to hear. The one that means a zombie has identified a human target.

'Braaains!'

The word rattles through the air like a rusty nail dragged down a dusty chalkboard.

Ace turns to the dune behind him, his heart in his throat.

There it is.

Perched at the top of the ridge, not a hundred metres away, silhouetted against the bruised sky, stands a zombie – gaunt, hunched and terrifyingly still.

'Braaains!'

The word grinds out of its throat once again, dry and splintered and soaked in hunger. For some reason, it's the only word the undead ever speak. Or, at least, it's the only word any human has lived long enough to hear.

Ace stares at the nightwalker with a cold, crawling terror. He can't tell if it's man or woman. Not that it matters. The undead have the strength of two living humans and the speed of the fastest sprinter, no matter how weak or frail they might have been while they were alive.

This zombie is all but mummified, its leathered skin pulled tight over sharp bones, cracked and peeling like old parchment, exposing blackened muscle that resembles beef jerky left out in the sun. Sand trickles out of it, as if the desert is now a part of its circulatory system.

Its face is a nightmare. The lips have long since shrivelled away, creating a mouth with a permanent snarl. Its gums are dry and grey, its tongue

withered like a dead lizard. It flicks across teeth that resemble ancient tombstones, yellowed and jagged. One eye has packed its bags and skipped town, leaving nothing but a crusted socket; the other is as dry and fractured as the sun-scorched earth, yet somehow it is still locked on Ace with a desperate craving.

'Braaains!'

This time it lifts an arm and points a rotted finger at him. The word is sharp and unnatural and tears through the silence like the rasp of a hungry vulture. Then the creature moves, at first with an awkward shuffle, each step kicking up a cloud of sand, its limbs jerking and twitching like a puppet tangled in its own strings. It looks like it's about to trip and fall.

It doesn't.

With every stride it grows steadier and more certain. Its pace shifts from the awkward shuffle to an ungainly jog to a full-out sprint as it hurls itself down the dune, arms pumping, mouth wide, teeth bared, its single eye locked on Ace as it ploughs across the hundred metres between them.

Heart thudding like a war drum, Ace moves. It's not a sprint so much as a calculated go-slow-to-go-fast dash as he circumnavigates the front of the old truck, each step a gamble between speed and stability. He knows that with one slip or stumble, he's dead meat. Or *undead* meat, actually.

He rounds the truck's hood –

Schrieeeeeeeeeek!

The sound is close and loud and savage.

Ace makes it to the driver's door. Hand trembling, he yanks on the handle and the door groans open. He throws himself inside, then pulls it shut –

Clunk! It bounces open.

'What the –?'

Schrieeeeeeeeeek!

It's even closer now.

Ace swings the door closed again.

Clunk! It won't shut.

He glances down. The seatbelt's retractor is busted, so it's dangling in the opening and stopping the door from closing. He reaches down and yanks it inside –

Then he sees it.

The zombie.

With jaws gnashing and its one eye locked on Ace, it rounds the front of the truck at a full sprint, its shrivelled feet slapping the ground like gunshots.

It's *so* fast.

Ace yanks on the door as the creature reaches for the handle.

Thud! The door slams shut then Ace slaps down the old-school manual lock.

Outside, the zombie wrenches on the handle and the truck rocks back and forth. Furious, the creature leans close and sniffs the glass.

'Braaains!'

Its voice is a twisted cocktail of appetite and rage. It tugs on the handle again, but the lock holds and the door stays shut.

Ace stares at the zombie, horrified and fascinated in equal measure. He's never seen one this close before. Time and decay have erased all detail of who this nightwalker once was. The skin on the left side of its face has almost completely rotted away, exposing raw bone and decayed teeth. On the right side is the empty eye socket, which makes it seem like Ace is staring into a bottomless abyss. What's left is a face carved by death that fills him with pity, revulsion and fear.

Ace's hand flies to the ignition. He twists the key and the truck's engine turns over – but doesn't fire. Panicked, he tries again. It doesn't work. Then he tries once more. No joy.

Then the zombie notices something.

The window.

It's open.

From when Ace wanted a little fresh air. It's only open an inch, but it's enough that the zombie can jam both its withered, black-nailed zombie hands through the gap and pull down on the window.

Ace sees it and his hand flies to the manual crank. The zombie snarls and pulls down on the glass as Ace winds it up. The window doesn't move but trembles under the pressure. For a second, Ace manages to hold the line as the winder squeals in protest, but the zombie is too strong. It slowly and steadily pulls the window down. And Ace can't do anything about it.

Two inches.

Three inches.

Ace takes one hand off the crank and twists the key in the ignition again. The engine turns over – but doesn't fire. 'Come on!'

'Braaains!'

The creature howls the word again, but this time it's with the gleeful anticipation of a delicious meal of human cerebral matter. There's enough space for it to slither its right hand between the door frame and the glass and grab at Ace's head.

'Jeez!' Ace ducks away, grips the crank tighter and twists it as hard as he can. With only one of the zombie's bony hands gripping the window, the crank turns more easily. Ace twists it hard, the glass rises – and pins the zombie's wrist to the top of the window frame. Only now does the creature realise what's happening and try to yank its hand free –

Too late.

Ace turns the crank one more time.

Crack.

The window slices through the creature's wrist like a transparent guillotine. Bones snap and tendons pop and the severed hand drops – and lands with a gross thud in Ace's lap.

The zombie lets out a howl and stumbles backward as Ace swings his hand and swats the withered claw over to the passenger seat, then twists the key in the ignition again.

The engine turns over – and fires.

'Finally!' Ace slams the gear lever into drive and stomps on the accelerator. The truck fishtails on the gravel then launches down the road.

Relieved, Ace glances in the side-view mirror to see the now one-handed nightwalker disappear within the cloud of dust behind them. He can't help but feel a little bit cocky. 'So long, sucker!'

His cockiness is short-lived.

The severed hand scuttles across the passenger seat like a monstrous spider and leaps towards him.

Ace's eyes go wide. 'You gotta be kidding –'

The zombie hand clamps around his throat and cuts him off mid-sentence, its leathery grip vise-tight and unrelenting.

With his left hand holding the steering wheel, Ace uses his right hand to wrench at the undead fingers that crush his windpipe.

For the life of him, he can't get the thing off.

Then the zombified hand squeezes *even tighter*. In an instant, all the air vanishes from Ace's lungs. He pulls his other hand from the steering wheel and yanks at the undead thing that strangles him.

It does not work.

He can't get it off.

His pulse pounds and his lungs burn.

The truck veers across the road. Ace pulls his foot off the accelerator to slow it down. In the side-view mirror, he catches a glimpse of the now one-handed zombie. It sprints towards the truck and shrieks:

'Braaains!'

But Ace doesn't worry about that because right now *he can't breathe*.

Darkness sweeps in. It rises higher and higher until it towers over him like a tidal wave – then crashes down and swallows him whole.

CHAPTER EIGHT

'MOVE your hands!'

All Ace can see is black.

But he can hear a distant voice.

'Move your hands!' The voice is sharp and urgent enough to drag him out of the darkness. His eyes blink open – just in time to see a long, glimmering thin shard of metal fly straight towards his face.

'Move your hands!'

He moves his hands.

Shlunk! The sharp, pointed tip of the umbrella slams into the back of the severed hand and skewers its leathery skin near the wrist. The hand spasms violently, its fingers snapping open with a sudden jolt that releases Ace's throat.

He sucks air like he's been holding his breath for an hour as a strident command reverberates from Cassie in the rear seat: 'Roll down the window!'

Ace doesn't need to be asked twice. He furiously turns the crank and the glass drops fast. As soon as it's half open, Cassie launches the umbrella out the window, with the writhing zombie hand still impaled on its tip.

Ace glances at Cassie as she slumps back onto the rear seat, exhausted by the brief exertion. 'Thanks, man. That was excellent.'

Cassie doesn't agree. 'Excellent? Excuse me, that was *awesome*.'

Ace smiles at that. 'Feeling better?'

Her face has more colour than before. 'A bit. I think the pain meds have kicked in.'

Ace rubs at his throat. The skin feels tender where the zombie's fingers dug in. 'Doesn't get much closer than that –'

'Braaains!'

The zombie is right beside the half-open window, grasping at Ace with its remaining hand.

'Jeez!' Startled, Ace stabs the accelerator. The truck leaps forward, kicking up a storm of dust as it leaves the creature behind.

'Braaains!'

Cassie watches the nightwalker shrink in the rear window and shouts at it: 'Yeah, yeah, yeah – brains, brains, brains. There are other words, you know.' She smirks to herself, then turns to Ace. 'Hey, what does a vegetarian zombie eat?'

Ace frowns. 'No idea –'

'Graaains!'

It takes a moment but they both crack up. The laughter cuts through the tension like sunlight through a storm cloud.

'Humour makes difficult situations easier.'

Ace agrees. 'Totally. Okay, my turn. Knock, knock.'

Cassie plays along. 'Who's there?'

'Interrupting zombie.'

'Interrupting zombie who –'

'Braaains!'

This time Cassie snorts so hard that she clutches her stomach in pain. 'Don't make me laugh!'

'Sorry.'

'I'm gonna lie down before I burst my appendix, which is exactly the thing I'm trying to *avoid!*'

'All good.'

With a wince, Cassie lies across the rear seat. 'Only wake me when there are more zombies.'

'If. *If* there are more zombies.' Ace hopes that one-handed meat puppet is the first and last one they'll encounter tonight, though, deep down, he knows the chances of that are pretty slim.

Ace drives on. The sun has gone and with it, their speed. Night has swallowed the road, so he eases off the gas. The old truck's headlights are dim and barely cut through the gloom. He can't see that far ahead, so every shadow feels like a trap.

He's not just worried about hitting more debris and shredding a second tyre. No, what really freaks him out is the idea of some hungry zombie darting onto the road, hurling itself through the windshield and landing in his lap. So, he drives slower than he'd like, never hitting more than eighty, his eyes wide open as he prays the road stays clear.

After ten minutes, something else slows them even further. In a flash, the wind whips up and a violent sandstorm sweeps across the landscape. The truck shudders under the onslaught as dust and grit mercilessly hammer the old vehicle. Ace quickly winds up the driver's side window and tries his best to peer through the wall of swirling sand ahead.

Then, in the rear-view mirror, Ace notices something glimmer through the storm. He looks closer.

What is that?

It's a single headlight.

Then he sees another.

And another.

In a flash, five pinpoints of flickering light slice through the billowing dust cloud, quickly growing larger in the rear-view. Then Ace hears engines.

They don't have the dull churn of a car or truck, but a raw and feral snarl.

Motorcycles.

As they draw closer, Ace's heart leaps with joy. Maybe this gang of bikers can help them. Maybe they can all drive to Larkspur in a convoy *together*. Maybe they have weapons to see off the undead if they attack again. Ace realises that's a lot of 'maybes', but he's just happy that he and Cassie are no longer out here alone.

The rising howl of engines cuts through the wind as the bikes tear towards the truck in a wave of chrome and exhaust. Ace sees them coming in the side-view mirror and cranks down his window. A spark of hope flickers in his chest as he leans out and watches the lead rider draw alongside the truck.

The spark of hope is immediately snuffed out.

These bikers will not help them.

Because they are not human.

Not even close.

What straddles the rust-bitten chopper to his right is a leather-wrapped horror – a weathered and decayed corpse held together by sinew and rage. Its half-shell helmet is cracked and sun-bleached, just like the twisted sneer stretched across its rotting face.

Ace has heard whispers about the 'smart ones' – zombies with enough brainpower to operate heavy machinery. They're super rare, apparently. Well, not *that* rare because five of them are now bearing down on this truck, riding choppers that look like they've just rolled through the gates of hell.

The lead zombie lifts a gnarled, accusing finger and points it straight at Ace.

'Braaains!'

Its voice is all gravel and cruelty. Ace responds by mashing his foot down on the accelerator. The truck jerks forward, its engine howling in protest.

'Hold on, back there!' Ace shouts over the throbbing engine as he glances back at Cassie, who shoots him a nervous grin. Ace looks back at the road and grips the steering wheel tightly, jaw clenched and eyes narrowed. His plan, and he's not even sure it's sophisticated enough to be called a plan, is simple.

Run.

The sand blizzard boils around them, alive and angry. It buffets the truck and whips dust and debris across the road. Visibility is a hazy blur and Ace can only see a few metres ahead. The truck shudders and groans as the speedometer's needle climbs. One hundred and thirty kilometres an hour. Then one-forty. And, finally, one-fifty.

Ace can just make out the outline of this road's solitary service station up ahead, the one that marks the end of the Crimson Dunes and the start of the desert. The big Shell sign isn't illuminated, so the place is closed. No-one works the night shift out here.

Behind the truck, the zombies' choppers blast through the sandstorm like desert wraiths, their engines snarling the bass rumble of a road demon. Ace's eyes flick left and right as he watches the undead bikers flank the truck. One thunders up to the passenger side, swinging a thick, rusted chain above its head like a medieval flail. With a guttural snarl, it whips the chain around one last time then releases it –

BRAAIINNSS

Smash.

The windshield detonates in a shower of razor sharp glass. Ace throws up an arm to protect himself. The jagged shards cut his hand but spare his face.

'There's another one coming!' Through the back window, Cassie sees a zombie rider, who's missing half its skull, veer in tight to the side of the truck. With its long, skeletal arms, it grabs hold and drags itself into the tray.

Ace catches sight of it in the rear-view mirror and wrenches the wheel hard left. The truck swerves violently – and the zombie loses its balance. It slips back onto its bike, which skids awkwardly on the gravel, then drops –

Crunch.

It's dragged beneath the spinning back tyres – and gets jammed under the axle. The truck bucks hard as Ace hits the brakes. The vehicle fishtails wildly – and its tyres catch on the gravel. Then gravity gives up and the truck tips over –

'Hold on!' Ace yells to Cassie as the world flips.

Metal screams.
Glass shatters.
And the truck rolls . . .

CHAPTER NINE

AND rolls.

The truck kicks up a storm of gravel and sparks as it flips over and over and over.

The zombie bikers don't have a chance.

Bones snap and limbs crack as three are instantly crushed beneath the tumbling wreck. Then the rear of the truck clips the gang's leader. He cartwheels through the air like the world's zombiest stuntman – then pancakes into the road with a resounding *thud*.

Meanwhile, the truck keeps on rolling –

Straight towards the service station.

Baaang.

It tags a petrol pump, then slams into the station's garage door with a teeth-rattling crunch. The thin metal folds like a soda can and the truck shudders to a stop on its roof.

For a long moment, there's no sound, except for the insistent tick of the truck's engine as heat dissipates.

Ace's eyes blink open.

The world sways.

His ears ring.

Dazed, he lifts a hand and touches his forehead. It stings. When he pulls his fingers away, they're slick with blood. He unhappily stares at them, then glances into the back of the truck. 'Cass?'

She pops into view. 'So, *this* is why you never drive to Larkspur after dark.'

Ace is very relieved to see her. 'You okay?'

She nods.

'So, in case it wasn't clear, we crashed,'

Cassie shakes her head. 'No, *you* crashed. I was just lying here minding my own business.'

Ace grins at that. 'Fair enough.'

‘What do we do now?’

‘We get out of here.’ Ace looks around then quickly understands that the fastest way to exit the vehicle is through the hole where the windscreen used to be. He gestures to it and Cassie nods.

Shards of glass glitter everywhere, so Ace moves carefully to avoid shredding his hands and knees as he crawls out. He helps Cassie to her feet and they take a moment to look around. Thankfully, the sandstorm has passed –

Bang! The garage door behind them flies open. They spin to see a towering figure blast out of the shadows and lurch towards them.

The duo recoil from the zombie – then it stops dead when it sees the wrecked truck and the trashed pump and the crushed garage door. ‘Who the hell did *this*?!’

He’s no zombie, though he has the unfortunately pale and creepy skin tone of the undead. In reality, he’s just some lanky guy in his late teens wearing grease-streaked overalls with a name tag that reads Trevor.

Ace raises a guilty hand. 'My b.'

Trevor's eyes move from the carnage to Ace. '*My b*? That's not gonna cut it, buddy. You trashed the whole place!'

'We were attacked. By zombies. On motorcycles.'

Trevor's not surprised. 'Of course you were. That's why you *never* drive to Larkspur at night. Don't you know this?'

Ace looks down, embarrassed. 'I do.'

'So, why were you driving to Larkspur at night?'

'It was an emergency.'

'What kind of emergency?'

Cassie answers. 'I have appendicitis.'

Trevor studies her. 'Look fine to me.'

'I took painkillers.'

Trevor is dubious. 'Should I call you a *wam*bulance?'

'I know you're trying to be funny, but *yes please*.'

'Everyone knows they don't make call-outs after dark.' Then Trevor squints at the duo. 'Wait, how old are you two?'

Ace answers. 'Twelve.'

'Wow. Sucks to be you, champion.' Trevor nods at the wreckage. 'You're in sooo much trouble. My boss is gonna go off like a frog in a sock when he sees this.'

Ace grimaces. He feels terrible. 'Yes, mistakes were made, but it was an emergency.'

'You said that already.' Trevor turns and walks away.

Cassie watches him go, confused. 'Are you leaving?'

'That's what usually happens when someone turns and walks away. My shift is over and this place is crawling with nightwalkers.'

'Can you give us a ride to Larkspur?'

Trevor shakes his head. 'Don't have a spare seat.'

Ace frowns. 'Your car doesn't have a spare seat?'

'I don't have a car because you never drive to Larkspur at night. I feel like we covered this already.'

Cassie is still confused. 'Then how are you getting out of here?'

Trevor points towards the side of the building. Sitting beside it is a stubby, homemade gyrocopter. It looks like the world's smallest helicopter and is basically a lawn chair with a propeller.

Ace studies the contraption. 'You're gonna fly *that*?'

'Last time I checked, zombies don't have wings, so it's the safest way to travel.' Trevor climbs in and flicks a series of switches. The engine coughs and splutters and roars to life.

Ace yells over the racket. 'So, you're just going to leave?'

Trevor yells back. 'Well, of course.'

'But what about us?!'

Trevor shrugs. 'Like I said, sucks to be you, champion.' Then he guides the gyrocopter off the ground. It wobbles into the air, then banks hard and buzzes away. Astonished, Ace and Cassie watch it disappear into the night –

'Braaains!'

Ace's eyes flick to the right, where a zombie hobbles towards the service station. It sees them and increases its pace from a walk to a run, though it can't move especially fast because it's missing a foot. Still, considering that inconvenience, it moves pretty quickly.

Cassie clutches her stomach. Ace sees it. 'You all right?'

She nods stoically, but the pain is written all over her face. 'Meds are starting to wear off. What's the plan?'

'I don't have a plan.' Ace glances around, then his eyes lock onto the wrecked garage door. Its metal panel has peeled back like a tin can, leaving a jagged hole. He peers inside – and sees something. 'But I do have an idea.'

Cassie follows his gaze – and sees the same thing. 'But is it a *bad* idea?'

'Only if it doesn't work.' Ace says it with a wry grin. 'And it's not like we have a ton of options.'

Cassie exhales. 'Okay.' She nods towards the garage. 'I'll handle that.' Then she nods at the zombie that limps towards them. 'And you handle old Stumpy over there.'

Ace grins. 'Now *that's* a plan.'

Cassie agrees with a smile that becomes a grimace as she slips through the hole in the garage door. Once she's gone, Ace turns to face the oncoming nightwalker.

His blood runs cold.

Now there are *three*.

'Where did they come from?'

The first is good old Stumpy, valiantly hobbling towards him. But the other two *sprint* towards him. They're about a hundred metres away, so he has maybe ten seconds before they arrive.

Swallowing his fear, Ace moves to the back of the truck, his shoes crunching on the shattered glass. 'Please be there, please be there –'

It's there.

The green metal jerry can.

It's dinged and scraped but still fastened to the side of the truck's bed. His fingers undo the latch and it drops into his hands. It's heavy. Not full, but there should be enough inside for what needs to be done. He unscrews the lid and an acrid stench punches him in the nose.

Gas.

Petrol.

Dino juice.

Whatever you want to call it, right now it's all that stands between him and the zombies. He steps forward and sloshes the petrol across the truck.

'Braaains!'

Ace looks up.

One of the sprinting zombies is faster than the others. It's seventy metres away and closing fast. The thing runs so hard, its feet barely touch the ground. Clearly it knows the early zombie gets the brains.

Ace upends the can until it's empty, then tosses it aside and dives a hand into his front pocket. He pulls out his grandad's old lighter. The one he keeps fully fuelled and in his pocket for a moment like this.

He flips the lid open with a metallic clack and drags his thumb down the flint wheel.

Ziiip.

Nothing.

No flame.

'Braaains!'

The fast one is fifty metres away now, its legs pumping hard, its mouth open in a horrifying scowl, its arms outstretched with withered fingers that resemble serrated claws.

Ace drags his thumb down the flint wheel again.

Ziiip.

Nada.

No flame.

Thirty metres away.

'Braaains!'

The zombie's solitary word promises just two things: pain, then oblivion.

Ace grits his teeth. 'Come *on.*' He drags his thumb down the flint wheel again.

Ziiip.

It does not light.

Twenty metres away.

The zombie's eyes are locked on him.

This is it.

Ace's final chance.

If it doesn't work, he's dead.

And so is Cassie.

And then he will be undead.

And so will Cassie.

Forever.

Ace's hand shakes as he drags his thumb down the flint wheel one last time.

Ziiip . . .

CHAPTER TEN

WHUMP.

An orange flame bursts from the lighter. Ace doesn't hesitate. He reaches down and touches the flame to the fuel-soaked pavement.

Thwump.

Ace jumps back as the ground and the truck ignite in a towering wall of fire that instantly rises between him and the charging corpse.

The zombie is running too fast to stop.

It plunges into the inferno and is engulfed by the flames. Limbs flailing wildly, it shrieks as its brittle, shrivelled flesh burns like tissue paper. It takes no more than ten seconds before it slumps to the ground, now just a roasted pile of twitching bones. The other two zombies watch the fate of their brain-eating comrade and instantly retreat from the searing heat.

Ace knows that he and Cassie aren't safe yet, not by a long shot, but this fire has bought them some time. A few minutes maybe, but when the flames die down, the zombies will be back.

Ace glances at the old Zippo in his hand. It sure did a nice job of lighting up that nightwalker. He grins and slips it into his pocket, thankful that the grandfather who gave it to him had been cremated and so could never become a zombie.

Ace freezes as he notices a river of fire race across the ground, from the truck towards the petrol pump it clipped during the crash. It gushes fuel like a severed artery.

'Oh no.'

Ace knows that under the gas station are tanks of petrol.

Giant tanks of petrol.

If they catch fire, well, that would be bad.

Extremely bad.

They would explode like a very large bomb.

Ace glances down and realises he's standing on the exact spot where the underground tanks are filled up.

He's right on top of the very large bomb.

He looks up and watches the fire snake towards the pump. They need to get out of there right now. He spins to the hole in the garage door. 'Cassie! We gotta go! Like, immediately!'

As his voice echoes, a low hum resonates. The second garage door shudders, then rises – to reveal Cassie sitting on an old four-wheel-drive quad bike. It's a dusty, faded orange and growls like an asthmatic lawnmower.

She glances over at him and grins. 'Let's roll.'

As she says it, the river of fire reaches the petrol pump.

Whump. A ball of flames erupts and howls upwards as fire spits and hisses from the pump like an angry serpent.

Ace recoils. 'It's only a matter of time before the tanks blow.'

Eyes wide, Cassie nods in understanding. 'Get on!'

Ace doesn't need to be told twice and bolts over to the quad. 'You okay to drive?'

Cassie nods though Ace can see she's in pain. He's happy for her to do it because he's never driven a quad bike before. His next-door neighbour had one, but his mother would never let him have a go because, she said, they have the unpleasant habit of tipping over and crushing their surprised drivers beneath them. Still, as he leaps on, Ace figures his mum probably won't mind him riding this one.

Crack. A jagged fissure splits the concrete beneath the quad's wheel as the ground heaves and trembles.

Cassie frantically twists the throttle and the quad leaps forward and races across the forecourt. The ground groans and buckles and another crack splits the cement beside them.

The quad thunders towards the road. It sounds fast but it isn't, really. Not that Ace cares. He knows it's quicker than running.

They clear the service station and zip onto Zombie Road, the quad's twin front lights throwing a pale beam in front of them. Their phones could do a better job of illuminating the night. But even though they might be weak sauce, the quad's lights are still strong enough to reveal what looms before them in the dark.

A wall of zombies.

They stretch across the road.

A hundred of them, at least.

Ace and Cassie stare in horror as the undead horde turns towards them. Then they speak. It's a chorus of voices, some deep and guttural, others high and broken, all rasping the same horrific word.

'Braaains!'

It echoes across the night like a choir singing the worst song ever.

Cassie slams on the brakes and the quad skids to a stop, tyres screeching on the gravel. They won't make it through that lot. Not a chance. That isn't just a wall of nightwalkers. It's a death sentence.

Ace looks around – then sees something to the left, in the far distance.

Lights.

Shimmering.

It's Larkspur.

The town they're headed for.

He points at it. 'That way!'

Cassie doesn't have to be convinced. She hits the gas, swerves the quad away from the zombies and aims it towards the desert and those shimmering lights.

The horde shrieks, then moves as one as they surge after them, a tsunami of rot and death and hunger.

One of the undead is quicker than the others. It breaks away from the pack and closes in on the quad.

It's twenty metres away.

Make that fifteen.

Ace glances behind them and sees it coming. 'Go faster!'

Cassie yells back. 'This *is* faster!'

Ten metres.

The zombie is *too* quick.

The quad cannot outrun it –

Boooooom!

The explosion behind them is colossal.

It's far beyond anything Ace could have imagined. The ground beneath the service station splits open with a thunderous crack and a wall of flame blasts out across the sand in a rolling wave of flames.

The undead don't stand a chance.

They are momentarily illuminated by the bright, orange flash of light – then incinerated in a cloud of ash and bone.

All except for one.

The zombie right behind the quad doesn't burn but is picked up and hurled through the air.

A split second later, the shockwave slams into the quad. The bike lifts, twists and flips end over end. Ace and Cassie are flung off and tossed into the night like a pair of rag dolls.

The heat hits Ace like a blast of dragon's breath. His skin sears and he's sure his hair is on fire. Then he slams into the ground, skids, rolls and comes to a stop with a low, ragged grunt.

For a long moment, there is silence.

Then Ace stirs. He's groggy. He has sand in his mouth. His ears ring. His eyes sting. His legs burn.

Hold on.

His legs burn?

He pulls himself up and looks down. Yes, his pants are on fire. He frantically grabs a fistful of sand and dumps it on the flames to put them out.

He turns to see Cassie, illuminated by the light of the burning service station. She lies sprawled on the ground twenty metres away, groaning in pain and at the edge of consciousness –

The fast zombie emerges from the gloom and stands over her. One of its arms dangles, dislocated from its shoulder socket. Half its face is peeled back like old wallpaper, revealing raw muscle and yellow bone beneath.

It stares down at Cassie and shrieks the only word it seems to know, that describes the only thing it will ever want.

'Braaains!'

Its jaw unhinges with a sickening crack, opening impossibly wide, its jagged, rotted teeth glinting in the fading glow of the fire. Ace had heard that zombies could do this, but until now he's never actually seen it.

He wishes he hadn't. The image is now burned into his brain and will stalk his nightmares for the rest of his life.

The creature drops to its knees and lowers its gaping mouth towards Cassie's head, ready to swallow it whole –

CHAPTER ELEVEN

'No!'

Ace doesn't hesitate. He moves fast, sand spraying behind him as he scrambles towards the zombie. When he's two metres away he dives and drives his shoulder into its side with all the power he's got. They slam into the ground in a snarl of arms and legs.

The zombie twists to claw at Ace's face with the fingers of its good arm. They dig into his scalp like hooks and yank his head towards its gaping mouth.

This nightwalker is stronger than it looks.

Much stronger.

Ace grits his teeth and pushes back, his arms

shaking as he strains to hold it off. The zombie's rancid stench floods his nostrils, putrid and sour, like roadkill baked in the sun. Ace gags as the corpse pulls him closer, towards the cracked black teeth that ring its horrible mouth.

Desperate, Ace flails for something, anything, to stop what's happening. Nothing his dad taught him about self-defence had prepared him to handle a situation like this –

Then Ace's hand brushes the creature's limp arm. He grabs its wrist and uses every ounce of strength to wrench it down –

Riiip.

The arm tears free of the zombie's shoulder with a spray of foul dust. Then Ace swings it.

Whack!

It slams into the side of the zombie's head. It doesn't let go of him, so he does it again.

Wham!

It still holds on. Ace's head is almost inside the nightwalker's gaping mouth now, so he swings the arm once more.

Thunk!

Third time's the charm.

The hit caves in the side of the undead's head and it loosens its grip. Slightly. For just a moment. But that's all it takes. Ace twists free of its grip, finds his feet and swings the arm again.

Slam!

It connects right under what's left of the zombie's chin. Its head pops free of its spine with a dry crack, tumbles through the air – then lands with a thud in the sand, its mouth hissing that cursed word: 'Braaaains.'

Its headless body doesn't flop to the ground, though. It blindly crawls away, towards the desert beyond.

Ace's hands tremble with adrenaline. He catches his breath then runs over and drops to the sand beside Cassie. 'How are you, my dear?'

'Just peachy, kind sir.' Cassie forces a grin, but it turns into a wince, and he can see she's in a lot of pain –

Schrieeeeeeeeeek!

A nightwalker sounds off close behind them.

Schrieeeeeeeeeek!

Then another.

Schrieeeeeeeeeek!

And one more.

The undead are coming, the rasp of their jagged voices slicing through the night air like broken glass.

Ace turns and clocks the shimmering lights of Larkspur in the distance. Then his eyes flick to the quad bike. It lies on its side in the sand about fifteen metres away. 'Let's go.'

Cassie nods and he helps her to her feet. She's slow to get up and almost doubled over in pain as they stumble towards the quad. Ace leaves her for a moment and grabs the vehicle to tip it back onto its wheels.

'Jeez!' It's extremely heavy and super awkward, but he uses all his strength to muscle it back onto its wheels.

'You can drive.' Cassie's voice is a whisper.

Ace nods and gingerly helps her onto the quad's seat, then climbs on. She wraps her arms around his waist and leans against his back. She is very hot and clearly running a temperature –

'Brains!'

The undead grow louder. Ace looks back – and sees at least five, sprinting towards them, their silhouettes clear against the dying light of the smouldering service station.

'Brains!'

He estimates they have ten seconds before the nightwalkers reach them. He takes a deep breath, presses the starter button, twists the throttle – and the quad roars away. Behind them, the shrieks of the zombies rise in a frenzy, then quickly fade, the sounds swallowed by wind and distance.

Ace drives carefully. The land between here and Larkspur is mostly flat, give or take a few dips and rises. But hit one ditch that's hidden in the shadows and it's game over. So, he keeps the speed up, but not so fast that he can't slam on the brakes if something unexpected appears out of the dark.

With the wind in his hair and Larkspur in his view, Ace does the strangest thing. He laughs.

Not because he's happy. Or relieved. But because laughter is the best way to flush out the panicked, anxious, jittery terror that's been coiled inside him since the sun set.

So, he laughs. In big, broken gulps. Because he's still alive. And Cassie's still alive. And he's even riding something that's almost a motorbike, like all guys named Ace should. And because, by some miracle, he might get to see his mum again.

He hasn't been a good kid lately.

There were nights when his mum would walk upstairs from the kitchen, exhausted from a hard day but wearing a hopeful smile, and just want to talk. She'd crack his bedroom door open and whisper his name, ask if he was awake. And sometimes he was. A lot of times he was. But he'd keep his eyes shut, breathing slow and deep, and pretend to be asleep. Because he knew what was coming. No matter how the conversation started, about school or friends or the state of this terrible world, it always came back to the man who left.

His dad.

And Ace couldn't do it anymore. Couldn't talk about him in an endless loop that went nowhere and resolved nothing except to remind him that they had been left behind. So, he would pretend to be asleep and she would withdraw and he would be relieved.

But now, out here, riding across this desert, shame sinks into his chest like a stone. He knows his mum deserves better than that, so when he makes it back, he will do better.

He'll be a good kid.

The lights of Larkspur draw nearer. It won't be long before they see the hospital's glowing blue cross –

The quad's engine coughs.

And sputters.

And dies.

The bike rolls to a stop. Ace tries to restart it.

It doesn't fire.

He screws off the gas tank's cap and gives the bike a shake.

No slosh.

No fuel.

No way.

They're out of petrol, stranded in the middle of a desert crawling with zombies, and a long way from where they need to be.

CHAPTER TWELVE

ACE'S jaw tightens as his heart sinks.

'What happened?' Cassie's concerned voice rises behind him.

'We're outta gas, Cass.' His tone is flat but inside he's freaking out, though he knows no amount of panic will magically refill the tank with petrol, so he keeps a lid on it. 'We're walking from here.'

'Okay.' She's understandably disappointed.

They climb off the quad and walk towards the cluster of lights on the horizon. Distant. But reachable. After a few steps, Cassie stumbles. Ace catches her then slips an arm around her waist, holding her up. Her body blazes against his side, even hotter than before. The fever's getting worse. He needs to get her to the hospital. Fast.

Still, she tries to stay upbeat. 'So, why did the kids cross the desert?'

Ace plays along. 'Why?'

'So the zombies don't eat their brains.'

Ace cracks a tight grin. It's not funny, but it is classic Cassie.

'Too soon?' she asks, tilting her head.

That makes him laugh. '*Way* too soon.'

She laughs too, and for a moment, the weight lifts off their shoulders. But just for a moment, because each step is a punishing slog. The sand is dry and treacherous and shifts beneath their feet. It swallows their shoes with every stride, turning the simple act of walking into a relentless grind. But Ace keeps them moving because stopping means death, and then a terrible *undeath*, and he isn't enticed by either of those options at the moment. He's not sure what would be worse: dying at the hands of one of these zombies or becoming one of them afterwards. So, he forces them onward, no matter how much his feet, legs, back and neck scream in protest. However bad he feels, he knows Cassie feels worse.

He wishes his dad were here, to help him, guide him, tell him it was all going to work out in the end. Ace often wonders if his dad is happy with the choice he made, if walking away from his family was worth it. Looking back, Ace realises the restlessness was always there, flickering in his father's eyes. Ace just didn't recognise it for what it was, didn't understand what it would mean to his life. He's not sure the anger of being left behind will ever leave him, but he does hope that, wherever his dad ended up, he's okay. That when the eclipse came and the world turned upside down, he was somewhere safe. Because the nightwalkers didn't care about maps or borders. They rose everywhere. In every city. Of every country. No place was spared.

Through the gloom, large, jagged silhouettes rise like forgotten giants before them, twisted and towering against the starlit sky.

Then they hear it.

The relentless, metallic clatter of a chain dragging a rollercoaster up an incline. The distant, broken tune of a calliope playing from a carousel. The rhythmic, groaning creak of a Ferris wheel turning slowly on a rusted axle.

Ace is staring at an amusement park. Then he realises something. Not only are the rides operating, but they are full of people.

No, that's not right.

They're not people.

They're zombies.

They're sitting in the dodgem cars that crash into each other mindlessly. They're crammed into the teacups that spin in dizzying circles. They're riding the rollercoaster with arms raised high and jaws open wide as they scream with delight.

No, that's not right either.

They actually shriek with hunger.

Ace knows this place. He's been here once before, years ago.

BE.

Before the Eclipse.

It's called Wacky Willy's Wonder World. Or was, back in the day. Ace came here on his seventh birthday and remembers it like it was yesterday. The sky was such an intense blue it made his eyes sting. He and his dad laughed so hard their cheeks ached, then they stuffed themselves with hot dogs and fairy floss until Ace almost hurled.

The highlight was riding the Death Coaster seven times (yes, it was called that before the undead moved in, because Wacky Willy thought it would 'scare you to death'). Ace remembers his dad wrapped his arm around him because he was nervous before the first drop, and that his stomach flipped as they plunged down the heart-stopping dip together, both of them screaming in delight as the world swept by in a blur of colour and light.

His dad even wore the T-shirt that Ace bought him for Christmas.

It said: *World's Coolest Dad*.

Of course, just wearing it probably meant he was the world's *uncoolest* dad.

The memories are so thick Ace almost has to brush them away from his face. Then it hits him.

That was his favourite day.

But this place isn't that place anymore. It's a rotting graveyard where, it would seem, the undead hang out when they're not hunting for brains. He wonders if they experience anything from being here. Is it scary for a zombie to ride a rollercoaster?

Ace has no idea. Most people believe that the undead only have feelings about one thing – finding and eating brains. They have no dreams, no memories and no feelings beyond a hunger that never ends. The idea that they possess an inner life, that they feel anything more than the urge to feed, has never been supported by any evidence.

Ace knows that he and Cassie must be cautious. The nightwalkers cannot find out that they're close. That means they should take the long way around so the undead don't have an opportunity to smell their brains. Ace points to the right, indicating they should skirt around this place. Cassie nods but says nothing. She's the worst she's been all night. Since the burst of energy when she drove the quad, it's all been downhill.

Ace tightens his grip around her waist. This is it. One final push. He powers forward, carrying her with him around the edge of the carnival. They move as fast as they can, ducking behind a large, crumbling building that Ace remembers well.

Inside is a giant funhouse called Clown Town.

The facade is now a grim smear of faded red and sickly yellow paint, blistered like sunburnt flesh. Above the entrance, a cracked jester's face grins in a frozen, silent cackle, welcoming brave kids in through its gaping mouth. When he was seven, Ace found the place terrifying – in the funnest way imaginable. He still finds it terrifying, but now there's nothing fun about it.

There's a straight shot to a flattened fence fifty metres away. Past that, a short stretch of desert leads into the heart of Larkspur, and then – the hospital.

Happily, there are no zombies in sight. Ace can still hear them shrieking on the other side of the funhouse, but he has yet to hear that one fateful word.

Braaains!

They don't know he and Cassie are there and that's exactly how he wants to keep it –

In the pale blue wash of moonlight, a tall figure steps out of the shadows in front of them . . .

CHAPTER THIRTEEN

THE figure doesn't shriek.

Or moan, 'Braaains!'

It stands ten metres away, still and silent, framed by the glow of Larkspur behind it.

Ace freezes and Cassie sags against him. Whoever, *whatever*, this is, it doesn't rush towards them. That alone makes Ace think it might be human. And if it's human, maybe it can help them. Get to the hospital. And avoid the zombies. That would be cool.

Ace narrows his eyes, trying to make out the figure's face, but the shadows cling to it like an old secret. He calls out, cautious and hopeful. 'Hello?'

No answer.

Ace glances to the right and identifies an escape route. There's open desert beyond the fallen fence. He subtly gestures to it and quietly says to Cassie, 'If this goes sideways, *we* go sideways.'

Cassie nods. 'Roger that.'

Ace swallows hard and looks back at the figure, his voice cracking slightly: 'Can you help us?'

There's no response. But still, no shrieking. So that's nice. He *much* prefers it when there's no shrieking.

Ace slides a hand into his back pocket and pulls out his phone. His thumb swipes it open and he taps the flashlight icon in one fluid, well-practised move. His pulse kicks up a notch as he raises the phone, the beam wobbling slightly in his trembling hand.

Then the light hits the figure.

And time stops.

Ace stares at the man with a face that once felt like home. He wears a T-shirt that's faded and frayed but unmistakable, with one simple message:

World's Coolest Dad.

Ace's breath catches in his throat. 'Dad?'

Sylvester Walker doesn't move. Doesn't speak. He just looks at his son blankly, distantly, like he's trying to remember the melody of a song he once loved but has now forgotten.

Ace steps closer. 'It's me. *Ace*.'

For a moment something flickers across Sylvester's eyes. Is it recognition? Or regret?

Ace's chest tightens. 'I missed you so much.'

Sylvester doesn't answer.

Ace stares at the father who left, then whispers: 'Why didn't you take me with you?'

There's no reply.

Then reality hits Ace. His father has been *here*. In Larkspur. This whole time. There was no grand adventure. He didn't go off to see the world. He was less than a hundred kilometres away. So close that he could have come and visited. Even after the eclipse. He could've returned to Red Rock and explained himself, instead of leaving his family in limbo, stuck between grief and uncertainty, unable to move on.

Of course, Ace doesn't say any of that. He doesn't dare. He's afraid one wrong word might scare his father away again. Instead, he asks: 'Why don't you say something?'

Sylvester's jaw shifts and his mouth opens – and a single word whispers through his cracked lips: 'Braaains.'

'No.' Ace reflexively steps backward. As he does it, the phone's light tilts – and reveals the truth.

The left side of Sylvester's skull is missing. There's just a dark, gaping hollow where his brain once was. From the look of the fresh wound, his father was turned recently.

Then Sylvester extends a hand towards his son, as if to say: *Come with me, we can be together.*

Ace feels a lump rise in his throat. For one terrible instant, despite everything, he wants to do it. He wants to go with the father he misses so much, the man he's thought about every day since he left.

'No, Ace. *No.*'

Ace looks at Cassie. The alarmed expression on her face says it all. He knows what she's thinking.

This thing in front of him isn't his dad. It's not the dreamer who picked him up early from school to take him to see the *Mission Impossible* movies or sang off-key to the radio when they went for a drive. It's something else, something terrible that wants just one thing. And as if to prove the point, Sylvester shrieks: 'Braaains!'

With a sickening crack, his jaw unhinges and stretches wide open as he rushes towards his son. Ace's instincts scream *move* and he obeys. He tightens his arm around Cassie then half-carries, half-drags her towards the flattened fence. Her fevered weight presses hard into his side as her fingers clutch his shirt front. The fence is maybe twenty metres away.

Halfway there, Ace realises they will not outrun the zombie that was once his father. Adrenaline surging, Ace searches for another option – then sees it.

Clown Town.

CHAPTER FOURTEEN

'CHANGE of plan!'

Ace spins Cassie around and they bolt for the funhouse. Sylvester instantly veers towards them and closes in with terrifying speed.

The kids round the corner of the decrepit building and burst into the funhouse through the mouth of the jester, their feet thudding against the warped wooden boards. Ace shoulders a set of swinging doors open then glances back to see if the zombie is following.

It is.

Cassie is confused. 'What are we doing?'

Ace answers as they rush along a narrow, claustrophobic walkway. 'We lose him in here, then sneak back out and head for the hospital.'

Cassie is not convinced by this plan. 'You sound very confident.'

'Well, "confident" is my middle name.'

'Really? I thought it was Stanley.'

They share a grin – then the stench hits them like a slap across the face: sour popcorn mixed with stale air, damp carpet and rotting fairy floss. It's a foul brew.

Suddenly the floor lurches violently beneath them, bucking like a tiny ship in a giant storm. They stumble and stagger and fight to keep their balance –

Slam! Wall panels burst open and giant clowns explode out of the darkness – jaws snapping, eyes glowing, arms grasping.

Cassie and Ace recoil as the clowns lurch towards them, laughing like deranged, cackling nightmares made real.

Click-clack-whirrr. The clowns jolt to a stop, hands jerking and mouths twitching.

Ace blinks, shocked. 'They're – animatronic.'

Cassie shakily exhales. 'Jeez, I almost peed myself.'

'Braaains!'

Sylvester's shrill voice reverberates close behind them. Ace hauls Cassie into a long, spinning barrel as warped carnival music cranks to life. Lights strobe and flicker while the tunnel twists one way, then the other, a vortex of motion designed to make you hurl. Ace grits his teeth and drags Cassie through it until they stumble out the other side –

Thwack!

A severed arm falls from the ceiling. Then a leg and a hand and a torso drop like grotesque pendulums, suspended by frayed ropes. One smacks Cassie across the face, another slams Ace in the chest with a meaty thud that all but knocks the wind out of him. The amputated body parts dangle and thrash, turning the corridor into a gauntlet of swinging, butchered flesh. Cassie panics and pushes one away – then realises it's just a prop made of silicone that's designed to horrify.

'Braaains!'

Sylvester is even closer.

Cassie turns to Ace. 'Where to now?'

'Down here!' Ace quickly leads her through The Amputorium and into a corridor. He knows the way. In fact, every twist and turn is burned into his brain from when he was last here. That's what happens with stuff you really love. You never forget it.

The duo sprint down the corridor, then blast through an entrance into a giant maze full of mirrors. There are hundreds and hundreds of them. Stretching from floor to ceiling and wall to wall, they turn the world into a gruesome kaleidoscope that contorts and twists their bodies.

Cassie's reflection is stretched sideways, her body pulled long and flat like she's been ironed against the glass. Her arms hang at strange angles, and her face is pulled wide with a distorted grin that reaches from ear to ear.

Ace fares no better. His reflection is compressed and hunched, his torso squashed and squeezed, his head way too small for his shoulders, with bowed legs that are weirdly stumpy. His body looks like it's collapsing under an invisible weight.

Then Sylvester appears in *every* reflection.

He charges like a beast unleashed, lips curled in a savage snarl, eyes wild with hunger.

'Braaains!'

Wham!

He crashes into a mirror behind Cassie and the impact rocks the whole place. Ace spins towards the creature that was once his father –

No.

It's just a reflection.

Then the *real* Sylvester blasts towards them. Ace yanks Cassie clear and the zombie slams headfirst into the mirror beside her. With a sickening crack the glass shatters and Sylvester releases a howl of rage, then turns and lunges at the duo – but crashes into another mirror that *reflects* them.

'This way!' Ace pulls Cassie through a door. They sprint down a walkway where the floor ripples like rolling waves while Sylvester's voice echoes behind them:

DAD

'Braaains!'

Ace and Cassie round a corner, then plunge down a steep staircase into pitch black. They reach the bottom and Ace snaps on his phone light. Breathing hard, Cassie squints into the gloom – and sees something. Her voice is doubtful. 'Are we going to . . .'

Ace nods. 'Yes, we are.'

They rush into the darkness. Using the light from his phone, Ace scans a control panel, flicks a switch, then another, then yanks a lever.

Seconds later, Sylvester barrels down the stairwell and stops as he scans the dark and sniffs the air, searching for the delicious scent of brains.

He peers into the murk as a harsh green light washes over him and the clatter of metal on metal echoes. Sylvester looks down – and sees he's standing on a pair of narrow, iron tracks.

Then a steam whistle rips through the air like a scream. Sylvester's head snaps around as the funhouse's ghost train bursts from the shadows with a hellish roar. It bears the blood-red face of a demon, twisted into a leering scowl, framed by razor-sharp horns that curl out from its skull with a promise of never-ending pain. Its twin headlights blaze fluorescent green, glowing like the eyes of the boogeyman who lives under your bed.

It races straight towards the zombie that was once Ace's dad. Sylvester barely has time to shriek before the train hits him square in the chest. Impaled on the horns like the saddest scarecrow, he flails uselessly as he is carried away.

A hollow ache twists inside Ace as he watches his undead father disappear into the darkness, the rattle of the train's wheels fading into silence.

Cassie looks up at her friend, her voice firm. 'That *wasn't* your dad. You understand that, right?'

Ace swallows hard and nods. 'Yeah. I do.'

But he doesn't.

Not really.

Not deep down.

He wishes he did, but that thing, that creature, is still his father, even if it wanted to eat their brains. Trying to reconcile the horror and grief of these two thoughts is enough to drive him cray cray, so he tries not to think about it. He wonders if he'll ever be able to get it straight in his head.

'We have to go. *Now*.' Cassie's voice pulls him out of his daydream. And she's right. There's no time to dwell. The demon train will return to this spot very soon.

Ace looks at his friend and nods. 'How are you feeling?'

She looks terrible, her face so pale it's almost green, but she forces a smile. 'Better now that we're not being chased by a zombie.'

Ace grins at that then loops his arm around her waist and helps her up the stairs. They retrace their path through the funhouse, then exit via the jester's gaping mouth.

There are no nightwalkers in the immediate vicinity as they double back around the building, navigate the flattened fence, then head across the sandy desert towards the lights of Larkspur.

They move as fast as Cassie can go, which isn't that quick. Still, she keeps pushing forward, driven by nothing but sheer will. She doesn't complain and she doesn't stop, but Ace recognises the pain in her eyes, and the way her knees slightly buckle with every step.

Then he sees it.

The hospital's blue cross.

It hovers like a glowing beacon above the city.

Adrenaline surges through him like a bolt of electricity.

They're *so* close.

Salvation is within reach.

'Do you see that?'

Cassie nods, the breath catching in her throat. 'I do. I see it –'

The ground shudders beneath their feet. Then the sand heaves and twists and ripples like it's alive.

Is it an earthquake?

No.

Skeletal hands explode from below, clawing at the surface with frantic, decayed fingers.

Ace freezes as the sick truth hits hard.

They're right on top of a zombie nesting ground.

And the undead know they're there.

CHAPTER FIFTEEN

A WITHERED hand bursts from the sand and clamps around Cassie's ankle.

'Ahhh!' The zombie's crushing grip is pure agony. She thrashes her leg to pull it free but the ground is like quicksand and she is quickly dragged down. 'Ace!'

He grabs her wrist and pulls with everything he's got.

It doesn't work.

In the blink of an eye, she is yanked down to her waist.

Teeth clenched, Ace pulls harder. He doesn't drag her free, but he does stop her from sinking any lower –

A zombie with a surprising shock of red hair blasts to the surface beside Ace. Coughing sand from its ruined mouth, it fastens a bony hand around his left forearm.

'Jeez!' It hurts like hell. Ace is jerked towards Carrot Top and loses his grip on Cassie. In an instant, she is dragged down to her chest.

'Braaains!' Carrot Top groans the word then unhinges its jaws with a sickening crack and lurches towards Ace's head with its mouth impossibly wide open.

Ace instinctively cocks his right arm, makes a fist, and drives it straight into Carrot Top's chest –

Wham! He punches a hole clean through its brittle, dry-rotted ribs, and the nightwalker crumples to the ground in a heap. Ace wrenches its hand from his arm then turns to Cassie.

Only her head is visible above the sand. 'Ace –'

Then she's gone.

'Cass!' Ace drops to his knees and frantically digs with both hands, sand flying in all directions.

His fingers tear into the ground, deeper and deeper – but there's nothing there except sand.

All around him, the dead rise, groaning and hissing as they drag themselves out of the fallow ground. Ace doesn't even look at them. He's focused on just one thing: finding his friend.

'Cassie!' he yells again, his voice ragged, his hands raw and bleeding as he digs like a madman.

Nothing.

There's no sign of her.

She's gone.

In that moment, something inside him breaks. Grief floods in, hot and wild, stealing his breath and blinding his eyes. He wants to scream her name again, but the sound dies in his throat, crushed by the weight of loss.

No.

He doesn't accept it.

He can't.

He won't.

He hasn't come this far to lose her. He dives his arms back into the sand and digs deeper, his fingers scraping blindly through the grit –

He feels something.

He latches on and pulls as hard as he can.

Cassie explodes out of the sand. She coughs hard and drags in a massive breath, the hand still clamped around her ankle but now severed from its forearm. She turns and looks at Ace. 'So, is *this* why you never drive to Larkspur after dark.'

Ace can't help but let out a short laugh as Cassie kicks the severed hand off her ankle. Still, there's no time to hang about as the dead crawl out of the sand around them.

'We gotta move.' Ace hauls Cassie to her feet and they run – or try to. For Cassie, every step is a war against the fire in her stomach. Ace claps his hand around hers and hauls her through the writhing maze of half-buried corpses, skeletal hands grasping and clawing at them as starving jaws snap open and shut like rusted traps.

With legs pumping and hearts pounding, Ace and Cassie weave through the zombie garden until they clear the last snarling corpse and charge onto open ground. Relief floods over Ace as they rush away, then he dares to glance back.

He wishes he didn't.

His stomach drops as the ground erupts in a full-scale zombie nightmare. Hundreds and hundreds of nightwalkers drag themselves out of the ground and shriek that one, horrible word:

'Braaains!'

The sound rips through the night as the horde charge after Ace and Cassie. They're just fifty metres behind.

Ace turns forward and sees the shimmering lights of Larkspur ahead. The hospital's blue cross glows above them all like a promise of safety.

And it's only minutes away.

The kids reach the road at the edge of town and finally leave the desert behind. They veer onto the main street and weave past parked cars and boarded-up buildings that have been expertly prepped to repel the undead.

The nightwalkers follow them, now just forty metres behind. Ace can hear their feet slap and scrape against the roadway in a grotesque rhythm.

He glances back and clocks two zombies who break away from the malevolent horde. They're faster and hungrier than the others and close in with a grim speed. The first is a withered corpse with its lower jaw missing. The second is a skeletal bride who wears a shredded white lace dress and holds a wilted bouquet.

Cassie falters and a pained groan escapes her lips. Ace keeps her upright and moving forward, ignoring the burning in his legs and the fire in his lungs. They turn down a narrow alley, its brick walls pressing in on them, then burst out onto a wide street.

There it is.

The hospital.

The blue cross shines above it.

It's so close.

Just a hundred metres away.

Ace spots a woman in scrubs behind the reinforced glass windows of the hospital doors. Whether she's a doctor or a nurse, Ace does not know, but she frantically waves them towards her.

Ace's chest tightens with a desperate hope. He glances back at the two zombies behind them. They screech in ravenous frustration and close in fast.

But not fast enough.

Seventy metres to the hospital.

Ace dares to believe they'll make it.

The doors to the hospital slide open and they can hear the woman in scrubs shouting to them, 'Run *faster*!'

Cassie answers: 'We're running as fast as we can, lady!'

Sixty metres.

They're going to make it –

'Braaains!'

A fresh horde of zombies floods in from a side street to the left like a tidal wave of rot, their eyes burning with a desperate appetite that will never be satisfied. They're only twenty metres behind Ace and Cassie.

And they're fast.

Too fast.

In a heartbeat, Ace understands the brutal math of this moment: he and Cassie are not going to make it. Worse, the nightwalkers will take them down right in front of the hospital.

Panic claws at his chest as his brain churns, searching for an answer to a problem with no solution.

Then he hears his father's voice, low and steady. It cuts through the chaos like a flare in the dark.

Go slow to go fast.

This time it's not a strategy. It's a choice.
And Ace knows what he must do.

He lets go of Cassie's hand and stops running.

She staggers on for a few more steps, then stops and looks back at him, her eyes wide with panic. 'What are you doing?!'

Ace turns and meets her gaze. '*Run.*' He then turns and walks towards the charging horde.

He'll go slow so she can go fast.

'No!' Cassie screams, but Ace doesn't look back.

Instead, he pulls out his phone with trembling hands and swipes it open. His thumbs hover for a split second, then he starts to type.

It's a message to his mum.

To say sorry. For sometimes being a bad kid. For ignoring her call. For what he did tonight. He hopes she can forgive him. And he hopes that she knows he loves her. That he always did, even when he pretended to be asleep.

He types fast, too fast, and the words get jumbled. So he tries again –

But now he's out of time.

The swarm of undead slam into him and the phone is knocked from his hands before he can finish. He tries to pick it up, but rotting zombies pull and grab at him and he can't do it.

Cassie stands frozen and watches it in horror. Then, through the churning mass of nightwalkers, Ace lifts his head. They lock eyes – and he roars the second-last word he'll ever say: '*Go!*'

It shatters Cassie's trance. She turns and sprints for the hospital. The zombie horde doesn't follow. They've found their prize with Ace. He fights them with everything he's got until he doesn't have any fight left – then they drag him down.

Through a narrow gap in the heaving mass of undead, Ace catches one last glimpse of Cassie as she stumbles through the hospital's entrance before the doors slam shut behind her.

She is safe.

A faint, aching smile flickers across Ace's face – then the dead close over him. He doesn't scream and he doesn't cry. He just shuts his eyes and surrenders to the dark.

LARKSPUR
HOSPITAL

CHAPTER SIXTEEN

THE low growl of an engine rises in the night. Headlights slice through the gloom like ninja blades – and illuminate Ace, who stands in the middle of the road.

Ace turns and blinks against the brightness as he sees the SUV approach. In the murky fog of his mind there's a flicker of recognition, like a match struck in the dark, for the person behind the vehicle's wheel.

His mother.

Diane sees him late and stamps on the brakes. The SUV skids wildly – then lurches to a stop in a choking cloud of dust, ten metres from where her son stands.

Breathless, she stares at him like she's seen a ghost, her face caught between hope and disbelief. Then she says his name. 'Ace.'

Ace tries to reply with 'Mum' but can't say the word. All that escapes his mouth is the only thing, he now realises, the dead are cursed to speak:

'Braaains.'

Ace watches his mum's expression fracture as she understands the awful truth.

Her son is a nightwalker.

Tears well in her eyes as her hands tremble on the steering wheel. Ace wants to tell her that he's okay, that she shouldn't worry, but he knows the words will never come.

So, instead, he raises his hands, brings them together – and presses them to his chest in the form of a heart. It's the same gesture he always makes when words are too hard. Hopefully, she will see that her boy, her good boy, is still here, and loves her.

For a frozen moment Diane stares at him, stunned, then, through her tears, she smiles and mirrors the gesture.

'Braaains!'

The terrible word rises in the dark. More zombies are close – and they know Diane is there.

Ace makes one more gesture. He raises his hand and points, for her to go, to leave this place – before it's too late.

He sees it in her face. She doesn't want to go. Every part of her is screaming to stay, but she knows the truth: there's no saving him. She holds his gaze for one, last, pained moment, then forces herself to look away. Jaw trembling, she throws the SUV into reverse and hits the accelerator.

The tyres kick up a cloud of dust as the vehicle backs up, swings around and speeds off. Ace watches the tail-lights shrink into the darkness, glowing like dying stars until they fade from view.

CHAPTER SEVENTEEN

CASSIE stirs beneath the hospital blanket. Her eyes flutter open. She blinks, slow and languid, as shapes swim in and out of focus before her.

One of the shapes moves closer as a voice, soft and steady and familiar, speaks her name. 'Cassie.'

Cassie's eyes adjust and she finds Diane, standing at her bedside with an expression caught between relief and heartbreak.

Cassie musters a faint smile. 'Hey.' The word is little more than a breath, lost beneath the low hum of the monitors nearby.

'The doctor said the surgery was a success. If you hadn't made it here when you did . . .' Diane doesn't finish the sentence. She doesn't have to.

Cassie knows what it means. Her eyes swim with tears, then she swallows hard and whispers, 'He saved me.'

The words land between them like something sacred. Neither of them speak. The silence is full and contains all the things they do not need to say.

Cassie reaches out and takes hold of Diane's hand and they share a broken smile. They'll always be there for each other.

No matter what.

CHAPTER EIGHTEEN

ACE is drawn back to the amusement park.

Once he steps through the rusted gates he sees the Death Coaster. It looms like a skeleton of steel and memory, its twisted tracks clawing at the night sky as cars thunder past, packed with the shrieking dead, their voices tearing through the dark like broken sirens.

Standing in front of it, still and silent, is Sylvester.

*

The Death Coaster approaches its first rise amid the groan of metal and the rattle of chains.

Ace's body is stiff and without breath or heartbeat, yet a familiar flicker of fear stirs inside him as the carriage inches higher and higher. It would seem that zombies *do* find it scary to ride a rollercoaster.

Sylvester sits beside him. He reaches over and wraps his arm around Ace. His skin is cold but somehow, it makes Ace feel safe, just as it did all those years ago.

The carriage tips over the rise and plunges fast, the track howling beneath in a blur of shadow and gloom. And in that moment, Ace knows, through all the rot and ruin, that he is not alone.

He will be with his father.

Forever.

WORLD'S
COOLEST
DAD

Watch out for more . . .

Dead Scary books . . .

Coming soon.